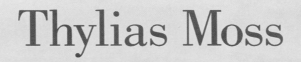

Thylias Moss

I WANT TO BE

pictures by Jerry Pinkney

Dial Books for Young Readers

New York

Today a lady, a man, another lady, another man, and my friend
asked me what do I want to be.
I thought and I thought. They were tired of waiting so I said,
I'll tell you tomorrow.

I walked home slowly. I kicked up rocks and dirt that filled the
air like tiny butterflies.

I held a handful of river water. Then I let go of it above my
head like rain.

I licked a patch of sunlight on my arm.
I played hopscotch in footprints after I made them.

I made a grass mustache, a dandelion beard, and a bird nest toupee.

The wind was a magician and it turned me into a dancer.
I danced until I was dizzy and the sky turned into a lake
so I stood on my head and was a fish swimming in it.

I double-dutched with strands of rainbow. Then I fastened the strands to my hair and my toes and became a fiddle that sunbeams played. Then I sang with the oxygen choir.

At sunset I was a firefighter and I squirted water at the
sun until it turned into the moon and until it was so dark
the stars couldn't play hide-and-seek anymore.
"All home free," I said.

By the time I got home, I knew what I wanted to be.

I want to be big but not so big that a mountain or a mosque or
a synagogue seems small.
I want to be strong but not so strong that a kite seems weak.

I want to be old but not so old that Mars and Jupiter and redwoods seem young.
I want to be fast but not so fast that lightning seems slow.
I want to be wise but not so wise that I can't learn anything.

I want to be beautiful but not so beautiful that a train moving
in the sun like a metal peacock's glowing feather on tracks
that are like stilts a thousand miles long laid down like a
ladder up a flat mountain (wow!) seems dull.

I want to be green but not so green that I can't also be purple.

I want to be tall but not so tall that nothing is above me.
Up must still be somewhere, with clouds and sky.

I want to be quiet but not so quiet that nobody can hear me.
I also want to be sound, a whole orchestra with two bassoons and
an army of cellos. Sometimes I want to be just the triangle, a
tinkle that sounds like an itch.

I want to be still but not so still that I turn into a
mannequin or get mistaken for a tree.

I want to be in motion but I want the ants in my pants to sometimes take a vacation.
Sometimes I want to be slow but not so slow that everything passes me by.

Sometimes I want to be small but not so small that
I am easy to miss. About the size of the thought
of a bud before it opens and becomes a universe
in which bees orbit like planets.

Sometimes I want to be invisible but not gone.

Sometimes I want to be weightless and floating on air, able to fly when I want to and able to stay on the ground when I feel like it. I want to be a leaf that is part canoe riding the water as if it's a liquid horse. I want to be comfortable in all the elements.

I want to be a language, a way to share thoughts. What my
grandmother says when she speaks in tongues. That's also music.
I want to be my other grandmother's hands, when she signs,
when she seems to be blessing everything.

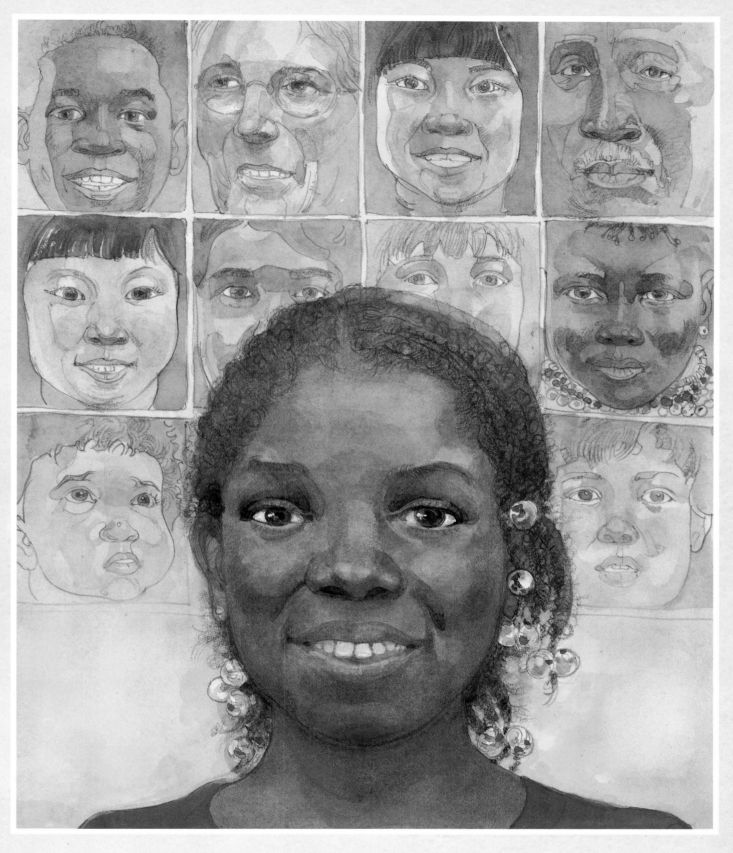

I want to be all the people I know, then I want to know more
people so I can be them too. Then they can all be me.
I want to be a new kind of earthquake, rocking the world as if
it's a baby in a cradle.

I want to be eyes looking, looking everywhere.
I want to be ears hearing, hearing everything.
I want to be hands touching, touching everything.
I want to be mouth tasting, tasting everything.
I want to be heart feeling, feeling everything.

I want to be life doing, doing everything.

That's all.

For Dennis and Ansted
T.M.

In memory of my mother, Williemae,
who encouraged me to be an artist
J. P.

Published by Dial Books for Young Readers
A Division of Penguin Books USA Inc.
375 Hudson Street / New York, New York 10014

Text copyright © 1993 by Thylias Moss
Pictures copyright © 1993 by Jerry Pinkney
All rights reserved
Typography by Jane Byers Bierhorst
Printed in the U.S.A.
First Edition
1 3 5 7 9 10 8 6 4 2

Library of Congress Cataloging in Publication Data

Moss, Thylias.
I want to be / by Thylias Moss ; pictures by Jerry Pinkney.
p.   cm.
Summary / After some thought a young girl describes in poetic
terms the kind of person she wants to be.
ISBN 0-8037-1286-3. —ISBN 0-8037-1287-1 (lib. bdg.)
[1. Growth—Fiction. 2. Self-realization—Fiction.]
I. Pinkney, Jerry, ill. II. Title.
PZ7.M8537Iaw   1993   [E]—dc20   92-28965   CIP   AC

The full-color artwork was prepared using pencil, colored pencils,
and watercolor. It was then color-separated and
reproduced as red, blue, yellow, and black halftones.